PUNISHMENT BY HOPE

ERIK HOFSTATTER

To Swim Dark Waters

TIM WAGGONER

"Reality is, you know, the tip of an iceberg of irrationality that we've managed to drag ourselves up onto for a few panting moments before we slip back into the sea of the unreal."

Terence McKenna

FOR ME, I THINK MY LOVE AFFAIR WITH THE TRULY BIZARRE began the first time I saw *Willy Wonka and the Chocolate Factory* (the original, not the Tim Burton remake). I watched it at home on television in the 1970's, not long after it was first released in theaters. It was probably some holiday or other, although I can't recall which one. (In those pre-cable, pre-VCR days, movies like *Willy Wonka* and *The Wizard of Oz* were only broadcast during holidays.) I'm sure I sat too close to the TV – I always did in those days – legs crossed and motionless, barely blinking, mesmerized by the story taking place in front of me. I empathized with Charlie Bucket, who wanted a golden ticket more than anything in the world, and I was fascinated by the strange, enigmatic, and more than a little frightening Willy Wonka himself. But what I remember most – and what had the deepest impact on me – is what's sometimes called The Scary Tunnel Scene.

Wonka has invited his guests, the children and their parents, onto a boat he calls his Wonkatania. They're going to travel on his chocolate river to another part of his wondrous candy factory, but to get there, they have to go through a tunnel. The trip starts out sedately enough, but once inside the tunnel, things start to get weird – *really* weird. The boat begins traveling at insane speeds through a kaleidoscopic nightmare-scape of rapidly-changing colors and disturbing images (including what looks like actual footage of a chicken getting its head cut off). As the Wonkatania races through this tunnel of horrors, Wonka begins singing a nonsensical song, face expressionless, his voice that of a serene madman. Toward the end of the song, he begins shouting the words, sounding terrified and on the verge of losing what few shreds of sanity remain to him.

And then, just like that, it's over. Wonka and his guests have reached their destination, although the trip has left them emotionally shaken.

That scene blew my preteen mind. I was already a horror fan, and I was well familiar with the various tropes in the movies I loved: monsters, ghosts, graveyards, full moons, mad scientists, haunted houses . . . The Scary Tunnel Scene had none of these elements, yet it was by far the most disquieting thing I had ever experienced. For several minutes, my head was filled with chaos and insanity, and I loved every second of it. As the years passed, I gravitated increasingly toward nightmarish, surreal, and existential horror, and eventually that's the territory where I planted my own flag as a writer.

So I'm certain it will come as no surprise that I *love* Erik Hofstatter's "Punishment by Hope." Like Willy Wonka's Scary Tunnel Scene, this story gets to the core of what makes the very best horror. Underlying both is the sense that the universe isn't orderly or benign, but rather chaotic and malicious – unknowable, uncontrollable, unpredictable, and above all, *dangerous*. In run-of-the-mill horror stories, characters are threatened with violence, injury, and ultimately death. But the mental, emotional, and spiritual wounds characters suffer can be far worse than mere physical pain. That's what makes The Scary Tunnel Scene so effective, and it's the thematic DNA of "Punishment by Hope." And the grotesque images invoked in each are both wonderfully repulsive and strangely beautiful. Erik's story is one hardly meant for children, though, and while the waters its hero swims are dark – *damn* dark – they sure as hell aren't chocolate. "Punishment by Hope" is an erotic, splattery fever dream of a story, as disorienting for the reader as it is for the poor bastard that's trapped within its pages. This shit is my *jam*, and if you're reading these words, my guess is that it's yours too.

So if you're ready – or even if you're not – take my hand and let me help you aboard. Your captain's name is Erik, and he's going to take you on a voyage you'll never forget . . .

No matter how hard you try.

———

Hell Is The Eyes of a Lost Lover

Her face was a broken mirror of rust-tinged waves. Nim swam through her eyes and mouth, breathing in angry droplets. She hissed at him with each stroke. The coppery taste of menses soaked his tongue. He stopped and peered across his scarred shoulder, bouncing like a stranded buoy. This was his life. His penance. To swim and carry. He knew the distance by heart. A tarnished box floated in a mariner's net tied around his waist. No other man on the island could survive her burning rage. His body ached. Not from exhaustion, but from desire to touch her. The sea smelled of freshly torn hymen skin. He pushed on, watery palms slapping him with perverted memories.

Sirilo paced the shore's end as wails of forsaken daughters sang in far-flung caverns. Nimlesh shut his blood-filled eyes.

Another sleepless night.

Tomorrow's promise fed him hope. He'd catch a glimpse of her again—if only for a darkened moment. He stumbled and crossed jagged rocks decorated with blackened tongues. The giant half-lizard observed, his reduced eyes calculating patience. His skin changed shades from red to orange and back to black in the bright star-fire that burned behind him. Nimlesh untied the net and removed its contents.

"You know, one of these days you'll tell me what's inside."

Sirilo flashed his little teeth and spoke in a human speech.

"Does it matter? Collecting these tins is the only way you get to see her."

Nimlesh bit his lip. It still tasted like menstrual tsunami.

"What if I wanted to speak to her?"

"Impossible. She tosses, you fetch. That's how it's always been."

His heart drummed a fast rhythm in protest—but Sirilo was right.

I swim and collect. Nothing more. But your eyes. They glow like wet stars.

"Stay behind the line and focus on your task. Get some sleep."

Nimlesh chewed on words spiced with vexation and resentment. He snatched his empty net and sauntered to the grave of the unknown mariner where eternal fire burned. The flames narrated a story if he listened hard enough. But not tonight. The grieving ship's solitary figure consumed all his thoughts.

She was short, but fierce. The wind tossed her hair like red sails.

What if the albatross line is your bluff?

A chance to speak to her was all he hungered for. To remind her how he felt.

Maybe if I shouted, the wind lords would deliver my words. But would you reply?

Nimlesh thought about her eyes—an aquamarine prison for his heart.

You're my sentence and I am yours.

Gruelling ocean labour tensed his shoulders and he fidgeted inside a structure built from whale bones. The daughters of promiscuous mothers still sang an agonizing chorus in the caverns above. Their voices ferried no words—only melodies, conducted by splintered souls. Their tears crashed and echoed on the glass cold ground. The sky was a dying bruise. There were no clocks—only passing moments. He wished for the hand of sleep to pluck him far from these strange waters.

———

The plateau shone like scales of murdered carps. Sirilo's old tails formed a breakfast tower near the unforgiving sea. Nim roasted and chomped on a slice. Flavour was a lost friend. He fed to survive. Life of a mariner branded him with a cruel fate.

We are who we are.

Hope walked hand in hand with him. She wore eternity's face and stilled his mind. A mist of veiled orphan eyes clouded his vision. The charred flesh crunched and blackened his teeth. Temptation invited him to lick flames.

That gift belongs to Sirilo.

Souvenirs of stolen kisses cut him like judgement shards. The grave.

Whose ashes...?

The grieving ship teased horizon's soul. A mariner's net hung from a protruding bone. Nimlesh tied frayed cord around his waist— a ritual of habit. He stood on shore's end, searing water eating his toes—but he felt nothing. Black tears painted his cheeks when gonads of castrated rapists rained down from the sky. The sea waited. Her fingers modified waves and they caressed his weeping face.

Nim swam closer and closer towards his heart—held hostage onboard the frigate.

Maybe you don't recognize me?

Sirilo was a shepherd of many.

Failure is not an option. I must cross the line. Just this once.

He missed the champagne voice flowing out of her mouth, where a colossal tongue hid behind walls of lustrous teeth—sometimes gently poking out when she spoke. Words smudged with a sweet lisp.

God. I ache for you.

The mariner backstroked for a nautical mile. A tampon-shaped cloud followed him, soaking his mind in crimson memories. He remembered when his tongue swam inside her menstrual cycles.

The albatross border—it's near.

More thoughts of her rushed in. How her face escaped from teasing words into the small dark world of her child-like palms. How her breathing changed when he quietly touched her.

Love handcuffs us to simple mannerisms.

Something brushed his hand. Nimlesh trod water, feet jaded but eyes alert. A white line of plaited albatross necks glimmered yonder. She hurled tattered rope from the quarterdeck. In the heart of the knot was an ancient box.

"Esiteri! Talk to me! Please!"

The rust-haired girl lifted her elfin visage. She was a pale ghost drowned in tyrannical waves.

Are you crying?

"Please! Esiteri! It's me! Say something!"

Silence—the cruelest weapon in your arsenal.

She pointed at the container. A ring with colours of the past decorated her finger. For endless nights he ached to feel her porcelain-smooth skin. To hear those sensual lips say his name.

Fuck the box and fuck Sirilo.

A deep breath entered his lungs and he vanished underwater. Pain ignited her eyes as he resurfaced on the other side.

"Don't be afraid! I just want to talk to you!" he shouted from below.

Fire teeth gnawed on her legs. Nimlesh gasped and drifted closer. The claws of inferno scratched at her torso. Pandemonium reigned. She washed in screams and flames, madly gesturing towards the border. They shared brain frequencies. He spun and crawled back behind the line. Esiteri was a renewed vision of defiance—ethereal and proud. Nimlesh blinked in rapid succession.

The closer I get, the faster you burn.

He submerged again to prove his theory. A crying sun melted her face when he passed. Nim retreated. Haste and desperation powered his limbs. He liberated the box and unfastened his net. The container floated like a steel corpse. A goodbye glance at restored beauty. Freckled skin and hypnotic eyes—a lagoon of blue intelligence. Delicate shoulders, quintessential hips. A work of art to be admired from afar. The ship cried large tears the size of human fists. They smelled like newborn sorrow. Esiteri nodded and his heart sank. He swam slowly back to the plateau, hoping to drown.

———

Nim sulked and listened outside the unmarked fire grave. She still screamed in the flame's echo. Snakes hissed inside his stomach. The island remembered nothing. He was a spit in a dark ocean.

There is more to life.

Truth eluded him. The madness began in the water. Always in the water.

That's where I was born.

A storm raged in his eyes.

My world is colourblind without you.

Seeds of change flourished in his soul.

There must be another way.

His head turned when a frustrated screech shattered his thoughts.

A brittle woman knelt in a small kingdom of collapsed bones. She reeked of despair and her fingernails licked dust off the ground.

"It's a terrible fate."

Sirilo's tongue kissed flames. He fed on fire just as his mariner fed on imagined love.

"What is?"

"Her task."

The half-lizard joined his side. He breathed through his skin, eyes glowing like falling embers.

Sirilo knows the inner mechanics of this island. Why things are the way they are.

"What is she doing with those bones?" he said.

"Those are the bones of her husband."

Nim peered at him. "What did you mean by task?"

"Don't trouble yourself. Think of your own, my friend. The ship is waiting."

Squalls of wind flung his hair. Rat kings chattered on the horizon. The magnetic sea pulled him closer.

"A storm is coming. I don't want to get caught and bitten."

Sirilo followed his gaze. "She's your greatest love. If you wish to see her, pain must be endured."

Agony drilled holes into the walls of his heart.

Your touch absent on my skin, my greatest pain.

"I must talk to her. Tell me what to do." he said.

A partially regenerated tail slapped Nim's shoulder.

"Communication is forbidden. All you can do is get drunk on her beauty. Those are the rules."

"Why?"

"Because truth kills hope. You aren't ready. You swim in ocean eyes of her grand illusion. The love you think you feel radiating from her soul isn't real. Her words will scar you, my friend."

Nimlesh leaned against a small boulder decorated with scalps of cancerous children.

Riddles be damned. My fingertips read stories, written in your skin like braille. You love me.

Sirilo studied his face, quietly absorbing thoughts.

"Her appetite for contradiction is insatiable. Tongue claims hate, eyes claim love."

"What do you mean?" Nim said.

"Your devotion is misplaced. She'll ruin you."

His skull was a dark field sowed with doubt. Nim's gaze shifted to the frigate and her ginger cargo.

"You question my devotion?"

"I question hers. You're not the first fool she caught in her web with a cheap smile. That magnetic energy. The vivacious mannerisms. She's a drug that makes you feel alive, I know. But you mean nothing to her. Beware of the chameleon who feeds on attention. She's always hungry. And she does not care who feeds her."

Nim sank teeth into his fist. "And what makes you such an expert on matters of the heart?"

"This swamp is my dominion. I am your shepherd—let go or she'll end you."

The mariner snatched a fishnet and waded knee-deep into the roaring sea. Then he veered.

"I'm not gonna let her go. You hear me?"

————

The wind howled and fought like raped men. Rat kings whispered poison in his ears.

What price would you place on my heart?

Waves of slaughtered ghosts held mirrors as he crawled. Esiteri's face.

Do you value me above others?

The sea was an angry lover dyeing black his reason.

Maybe I am a fool.

Nim swam faster and faster whilst water claws tugged him down. The albatross border, drowned martyrs. He was a broken passenger on shoulders of old waves. Esiteri glared from her wooden prison.

She flashed a hollow grimace, lips painted with lamented shades.

In her sylphlike fingers she clutched a bloody square. Thigh skin—a parting lover's final gift.

Nimlesh drank in shapes of her curves.

Remember my tongue inside you, your body singing in fluids?

Eyes stitched with sorrow watched him. A mystifying jellyfish fed on the surface.

"Are you alright? Talk to me." he said.

Odium thrived on the skin piece as she wrote. Nim waited for dead answers resurrected by her hand. Then his body screamed in agony.

"What are you doing? Stop."

The water reflected scorn. Esiteri carved more words. He was a red speck in a circle of fish tears.

"No more, please."

She nodded and threw a box overboard—another silent thorn in his heart.

Hold me...

A net trapped her concealed emptiness.

Is that what you are?

———

In depths of her soul he found blind intimacy. Tangled words and dying time. She floated inside his veins.

Together we crumble like Jupiter dust.

Nimlesh read crimson letters earned with pain. Fire hands rubbed his back. YOU ARE HORRIBLE. YOU ARE TOXIC. I HATE YOU. Three lines stamped on three ribs.

"I warned you..."

The enflamed grave housed his shadow. Sirilo juggled whale bones. A coy smile dominated his face.

"...that her words would scar you."

Nim dressed himself in defiance and glared at the shepherd.

"You know nothing about what happened."

"I don't need to. I can read for myself what she thinks of you."

His eyes pushed out newborn tears.

"You don't understand the rules of her game. She wants me to be unsure. To keep me off balance. She likes to think nobody gets through her layers, but I did."

"Nonsense. You're horrible and toxic. She hates you." Sirilo said.

Her words gushed from his tongue like poison. He hunted for clarity in a cloud of unfamiliar darkness.

"Esiteri is a complex and stubborn design, but I know she loves me."

Sirilo circled him. "And I know there's no love in that empty heart. Your weakness amuses her."

Beyond the bridge of broken spines, the woman bone-builder still knelt in her melancholy.

"Our souls are stitched together. Her willingness feeds my hope."

"Willingness for what?" Sirilo said.

Nim faced the bridge. "To swap words."

———

An orchestra of jellyfish sang somewhere in the water.

A lament for lost lovers.

Red dust smothered his feet as he sauntered to a luminous cavern. She still knelt in a maze of bones—her home.

"What are you doing?" Nim said.

The woman raised her eyes that pierced souls with sharp intelligence.

"I'm building a ship."

Curiosity pushed him closer. He peeked over her pygmy frame. She smelled liked white florals and vanilla and hidden tears.

"Why are you building a ship from bones?"

"Because that's where she is."

Suspicion narrowed his eyes. She had a delicate nose and her lips reminded him of violet clouds.

"What's your name?"

"Kalara. I am the keeper of the albatross border."

Nim's heart wrinkled.

I can't pass because of you.
Malice entered his voice.
"Why are the bones charred?"
Her face was a veil of wet sadness.
"When you cross the line, I set her bones alight."
"Why?"
"When they burn, she burns."
His fists trembled.
"Yes, but tell me why?"
"She destroyed us, so I'm destroying her."
I don't even know you. Why are you like this?
"I'm not following, Kalara. What do you mean she destroyed *us*?"
A vision of untamed nails fostered by neglected days.
How long have you been a keeper?
The wind roared in his face like a waking lion.
"She's so cruel. Her tongue ever so vicious. But you relish the pain. Attraction and destruction."
"I'm confused…" he said.
Kalara was a calligraphy of freckled sorrow hanging in a bone shipyard.
"She's a serpent who bites with dismay, but little doses of her venom entice you. That's how she controls your emotions. You *must* surround yourself with people who have the same heart as you."
"I don't understand…"
"You crave validation from an emotional shredder." Kalara said.
The red earth beneath their feet disagreed.
"What's going on?"
"The giant fish is stirring and causing quakes."
They held hands in loud terror.
"Stirring where?"
"At the bottom of the empty ocean."
The tremor ceased when he thought of her melody.
If you get lost in me, just follow the stars to my heart.
"Sirilo gifted you with verbal arrows, but you both missed."
Kalara pointed at his ribs. "The truth is written on your skin."

———

He sauntered to the plateau, melancholy sagging his shoulders.

You locked your heart away in a cage—too afraid to let it loose.

"And the key is beyond your reach."

Nimlesh veered and his shepherd indicated to the nebulous caverns.

"The wailing women and their unrelenting suffering."

"Aren't you curious why they suffer?" Sirilo said.

Their cries rolled down like boulders of despair. Nim shielded his ears.

Too many tears. Too many sorrows.

"Tell me."

His mouth twisted in a sly angle. "Come, I'll show you."

The ground was littered with simian nails, his palm brushing against a red-stained wall.

The colour of you.

A fragmented memory struck him. His fingers raked hair in a ginger garden as she dosed on his chest. Her trust, absolute. The moment he wanted to relive again and again.

I miss your scent, cheap soap and dirty kisses.

Sirilo motioned to a trinity of transparent bottles and the crying women who dwelled inside. Dread corkscrewed his organs. They were shackled in torment. He gasped when their palms overturned.

Aquamarine eyes…sewn into them.

"What the hell?"

The half-lizard dissected his reaction.

"Hell is the eyes of a lost lover, forever gazing back."

Nim forgot how to blink. "What's the purpose of these women?"

"Their songs serve as reminders," Sirilo said to his captive sirens.

"Reminders of what?"

"What broken hearts truly sound like."

"But why eyes of their lovers?" Nim said.

Sirilo shrugged his reptilian shoulders.

"The betrayers. They fell through her window—and she dismantled them."

Nim felt queasy, like his heart was being crushed by coarse hands.

"Her window?"

"They say that eyes are windows to our soul, yes?" Sirilo said.

He nodded, chewing on impending warnings.

"Leave her window closed."

————

She roasted in the belly of flames, voiceless and beautiful—even in her suffering.

I want to feel the heat from your skin, to warm my hands on your energy.

Betrayers wept in glassy caverns, but paradisal thoughts soaked him like petal rain. Nim's eyes came alive with sudden realization—a bite of clarity. The bridge of broken spines. Kalara's domain.

If I stop her from burning your bones…

A thunder of hope struck his heart. Esiteri was a broken compass pointing to misleading contradictions. An enigma of missing letters.

I promise to decipher the blind alphabet living in your eyes.

Echoes of aborted embryos spilled from the ink-dark sea. He walked fast, evading pleas. Shadows hitched a ride on his back and ashes painted his feet in fossil grey. Nim hesitated on the bridge. She slept among naked bones, her face cold as a porcelain lake. He wrapped his fingers around a jagged stone.

"You came to murder me?" Kalara said.

Nim relaxed his grip. "I need your help."

"I know what you will ask of me, but we must bond first."

She sauntered nearer, her steps nimble and elegant. Kalara tore a hole in her fishnets. A short white string dangled between her thighs.

"What are you doing?"

The keeper drew out a tampon, staining his face with curious lust. She slid a finger deep inside herself.

"Taste me."

Nim obeyed, sucking blood from the tip of her finger. Then he drank more from the red fountain that was her tidy cunt. She tasted like bleeding heaven.

"Right there. Lick me clean."

Kalara moaned, but suddenly shoved him aside.

"Did I not please you?" he said.

"Pleasure is not the objective."

"And what is?"

"The unbreakable bond we just gave birth to. Kiss me."

When she closed her eyes, he kissed her head with a fistful of stone.

"Loopy whore."

———

Knee-deep in black water, he pondered. The grieving ship teased him from a darkening horizon. Nim's face hosted a carnival of triumph.

Your arms, my shelter.

Sirilo judged his deeds from a shadow grave of the unknown mariner. His tongue consumed flames, his eyes drank folly. Nim plunged beneath the waves, then resurfaced riding a giant blood-soaked tampon. He paddled with frantic speed, arms refueled by unleaded desire.

The guardian of plaited albatross necks was an unconscious threat. Angry swells steered him closer. Red was the colour of his destiny. He smirked.

I'm coming for you.

Something tucked at his foot. Tuck. Tuck. Wet hair obscured his vision. A jellyfish floated on the surface. It winked with a stolen eye and vanished again.

When he resumed paddling, a powerful tentacle dragged him under by the ankle. Nimlesh breathed out a bubbly crown. He sank deeper and deeper like an anchor of meat.

She brought him inside a cavernous kingdom. Nim sprawled and coughed on a platform smeared with a thousand foreskins. The jelly-fish's saucer-like body morphed into a humanoid figure.

"W-what are you…?" he said.

"Torika."

That voice…a female owner.

Torika hopped on little tentacle feet, tittering. He remained vigilant and scanned his new world. A queer luminous fluid leaked from stone giant's wounds, enshrouding the cave in purple light.

"Where are we?"

Teardrops landed on the cape of his neck. A crab squad marched a heart formation around him. Nim shrank and hugged his knees.

An underwater kingdom ruled by a jellyfish queen and her army of crabs.

His eyes widened when the sea turned purple.

"What do you want?"

Torika whistled and her slaves retreated. She pointed at his chest.

"You want my heart?" he said.

"No, silly. I want your garments. They're soaked. Take them off."

More foolish tittering. He felt sheepish. Exposed.

"You can dry them here, look." Torika said.

She gestured at piece of flat stone. Nim shed wet fabric like old skin and jumped off the platform. The stone hissed a warning in a dead language.

"Don't be afraid. He likes you."

Nimlesh's gaze travelled to her, then back to the breathing stone.

"What is this place? Why am I here?"

She read the scars on his ribs. Her transparent body was a vessel for human eyeballs. They flowed inside her.

Who are you?

The glass sirens and their punishment. Were they connected?

Hell is the eyes of a lost lover, forever gazing back.

"I brought you here because you need my help."

"Help with what?" he said.

"Esiteri—your lost lover."

Her name sounded dirty when she said it, like it was dragged through mud.

"Why would I need your help?"

Torika tittered again. "Can't you read? She hates you."

"Anger is merely her shield. Why do you care what she thinks of me anyway?" he said, teeth gritted.

The stone objected to his tone, hissing a louder warning. A legion of crabs mustered behind her.

"Lower your voice. I don't think you understand. Esiteri is a half-drawn map. She'll set you on a path, but if you want to find her heart —you'll need me to lead you to it."

"I know who she is and what she wants."

"She slept with you, yes, but was never yours. Was she?"

Torika regurgitated three eyeballs, then fed them to her slaves. Nim averted his gaze.

"Is it disgust that makes you look away, or the truth?" she said.

A bloated crab slept beneath her tentacles.

"I lit up her world once, but now I'm a dying firework. That's all I ever was."

"I know your thirst for her nectar is unquenchable."

He said nothing.

"Forbidden fruit tastes the sweetest. If only you threw her away after a bite, but you craved more."

"I wanted to devour her. Again and again."

A passionate flashback eclipsed his heart. Hard hands dipping into her lily-white ass. Daring eyes and urgent whispers. *Fuck me, daddy.* His thumb exploring the smooth pink jewel as he rammed her from behind. And those generous lips—stained with colour of his unborn children.

"Poor Kalara."

That name fractured his reverie. "Kalara? The keeper?"

"She is your wife." Torika said, chortling.

The crabs repositioned themselves into a K shaped letter.

"I don't have a wife."

"You do. She's out there all alone, building a ship from bones. Her husband's bones—your bones."

The hands of disbelief turned his head side to side.

"I don't believe you. Those bones belong to Esiteri. She burns them out of jealousy. To stop me."

Torika spun like a drunken ballerina, unleashing mocking waves of laughter.

"And why do you think she's jealous, silly? Listen to yourself."

He pressed his temples, eyes darting to the water.

"Return me to the surface. I don't want to hear more of your lies."

"As you wish. But remember this: she led you inside her vagina, but only I can lead you inside her heart."

Torika resumed her true jellyfish form and coiled a tentacle around his wrist.

———

The albatross border shimmered behind him when he breached. A rope ladder hung from the frigate's side. Salty waves hummed cryptic warnings. Nim swam closer. He gripped the rungs and climbed onboard. A deserted hull greeted him. No crew—only uneasy silence. Parched floorboards sucked droplets from his toes. He skulked along the flush deck and there she lingered. A haunting melody of pale notes.

"Esiteri?"

She veered. Her hair blew wild like a red cyclone.

"You shouldn't be here."

"I just want to talk to you," Nim said, palms facing her—inviting embrace.

The sky changed colour like reptiles of the old world. A half-eaten whale carcass thumped against the underside. Esiteri's countenance was a stone tablet carved with symbols of unknown origin. He swallowed, eyes struggling to read the face he knew so well.

"There's nothing I want to talk about."

She perfected her little tortures and wore her favorite mask of cold indifference.

"Please...we've done this dance before." he said.

"I appreciate you trying, but you're not right for me."

Nimlesh chewed on her words, head bowed.

"How can you say that to me now? After everything. I love you."

"After everything," she scoffed, "we slept together three, four times. I only knew you a year."

Mouth agape, his knees buckled. Those verbal splinters bled him slowly.

"Are you telling me that I was your experimental sex toy? So cruel."

"Sometimes you have to be cruel to be kind."

Sirilo's phrase bounced between his brain walls.

She's an intelligent chameleon.

Nim speculated if she was camouflaging her true feelings now, or if she showed specific shades of herself she knew he'd like—only to seduce him.

"That magnetic field in your eyes made me stick to you like cobalt. My heart fell into you. Then you changed. Now your eyes remind me of a dead mackerel. Why?"

Esiteri frowned. "I liked you. I thought you were a greener pasture, but you didn't make me happy."

Frustration sculpted his face into an ugly grimace. "You gotta take the good with the bad, darling."

"But what if the bad outweighs the good?" she snapped.

Nim licked his salty lips. She was immune to reason when stubborn anger burned inside her veins.

"I'm not gonna let go."

"Forever blind to all your wrongdoings. Don't you see that I need someone who compliments me?"

Nim flashed his ribs. "Read my scars. You don't earn compliments with vicious words."

"Always playing the victim. You repel me."

"Just listen to yourself. Taste the poison before you spit it at me."

"I *hate* you and your toxicity, that's the problem." she leered.

Furious atoms clashed inside his body. Gold chains decorated her petite throat and he imagined coarse hands around her neck—bringing a deathly chain of human fingers to her collection.

"Stop being so volatile. I can't just shut you out of my heart."

"I'm so much happier when we don't talk."

Nim rubbed his forehead, pushing back desperation.

"We're wildfire together. Let's move on, yeah?" Esiteri said, eyes harder than marble. Then she pushed him overboard and he sank back into the water and even deeper into the ruins of his heart.

———

Sirilo curled on the burning grave, his rapid tongue thrusts gathering flames. Nimlesh envied his casual detachment and love-free existence.

I swim and collect. Nothing more.

He tapped his temples on a chair carved out of whale bones.

"You can't rekindle that flame, my friend. Not in your current form anyway."

"What do you mean?" Nim said, eyes wide and alert and brimming with perplexity.

The half-lizard changed position in the mouth of inferno.

"You represent an identity that temporarily attracted her, but she belongs to a family you'll never be part of. She will always remain loyal to them."

"Family? What are you talking about?"

"She's been yo-yoing you for a year. Cut the string, my friend." Sirilo said.

Nim paced in endless circles around the grave.

"I lack the strength to resist those round blue magnets. They pull me in."

"Let her go."

"No. Our love is higher than reason. Higher than wisdom. Higher than God."

The shepherd urinated on Nim's shadow from a banquet of embers.

"Delusional thinking. The woman *hates* you. Focus on your wife."

The second mention of "wife" derailed his train of thought. "I never married anyone."

"You married Kalara."

He veered and faced the humanoid reptile.

"Why are you cahooting with Torika? What did she tell you?"

"I don't know that name." Sirilo said.

Nim jabbed his finger into the moist shoulder skin.

"You know who she is. The jellyfish hybrid child thing that lives beneath the albatross border."

The half-lizard's snout expanded.

"The Mother of Crabs dwells down there. That's her domain. This creature…what did it want?"

"Nothing. She force-fed me lies."

"Those waters are deep, my friend. Forget the black ship. Kalara grieves for you."

Nim gnawed his right knuckle, suppressing rage.

"Kalara means nothing to me."

"She should. She's your wi—" a fist collided with teeth. Nimlesh sprinted seaward.

"Where are you going?"

"You know where. If you can't help me win her heart, then maybe she will."

"Don't—everything will change." he shouted, but his words fell on deaf waves.

———

The sky cried rotten grapes. His arms punctured combers like fleshy spears. A reel of half-cut thoughts weighed him down in a mantric sea. It whispered to him.

Kalara is not your wife. Kalara is not your wife. Kalara is not your wife.

Somewhere on crest of waves, a chameleon dressed in eyelashes gave birth to a red star.

"To-ri-ka! To-ri-ka!" he shouted, hands cupping sides of his mouth.

A tentacle caught his attention, then his foot. Nim savoured last breaths and thought of dying moons in a sleepless kingdom. She pulled hard. In the underwater plains, in a circle of enslaved crabs, meditated a one-armed girl with floating black curls. He closed his eyes as the pulsating bell accelerated faster.

"Breathe."

The cave sweated purple haze from its walls.

"Are you the Mother of Crabs?" he said, gulping for stale air.

"Where did you hear that name?"

"This is her domain, according to Sirilo. Who is she?"

"She is my sister. Did he not also tell you of Enola & Aleš?"

"No. Who are they?"

"That is a story for another time. Why did you seek me in the sea?"

Nim perched himself on a pincer-shaped rock. The rash forming on his ankle seemed identical to Esiteri's emblematic ring.

"I had to find you—you must help me."

Torika tittered. "She rejected you. Do you know why?"

"Because she belongs to a family I'll never be part of?" Nim said, repeating borrowed words.

"And do you know *why* you'll never be part of that family?"

Nim scratched his ankle. "There is no family. She lives and grieves alone on that vessel."

"No, there are two others. You can join them, but not in the body you presently occupy."

"What do you mean?"

"Your organs are wrong." Torika said, drawing heart-like ripples with her thin arms.

He scoffed, patting his chest and abdomen. "They are where they should be. I don't understand."

"The acidity of these waters can help you transcend. To become more than you are now."

"I know who I am. Why would I want to be more?"

Torika released her internal glow. The bioluminescence sprayed his face with persuasive light.

"Look at me. I don't own a brain or a heart. These eyes are stolen. Focus not on the perception of yourself, but on the perception of others. What matters is how Esiteri sees you. That is why you are here."

Nimlesh pursed his lips, deflecting desperation.

"Are you telling me that I must become someone else for her to love me?"

"I know you're stubborn and would rather be hated for who you are, than loved for who you are not but believe me—this is the only route to her heart."

"What must I do?" he said, jumping in the water beside her.

A small zoea crab slept on her slender limb. "Lean back and open your mouth."

"You want me to eat that?"

"Only if you wish to be with her. The choice is yours."

————

He slept in a seabed for what felt like days, dreaming of landscapes painted by red pincers. A platoon of crustaceans tailored his flesh. Nimlesh screamed in a higher octave. He broke water and sprawled on a rock. His skin colour changed.

"What have you done to me?"

The voice was not his own. He sniffled and whimpered—unrecognized characteristics. Nim hammered shrunken fists against stone, breeding emotions six shades of vulnerable.

"What is happening?"

Torika drifted closer on a trail of vortex rings.

"The metamorphosis you asked for."

Nim spasmed and cupped his groin.

"It hurts…"

She stung and paralyzed him with a dance of furious tentacles.

"W-what are you doing?"

"Easy. You are Nina now. I'm rewiring you by turning off genes that maintained your testis. I'm creating a whole new genetic pathway, you see. This chain reaction will turn on oestrogen in your body—so your new ovaries can form."

"Nooo…w-who are you?" Nina said through gritted teeth, her cheek bones slowly reconstructing.

"Think of me as an organ engineer. I'm reprogramming your cell memory towards a female fate."

"But why?"

"Esiteri grieves for a long dead partner. A female partner."

Nina gazed inside a water mirror. A reflection pregnant with newly-fashioned possibilities.

"You now represent everything she's lost, but you mustn't reveal your true self."

"You want me to live a lie?" Nina said.

"I want you to learn her constellations."

———

She swam inside a storm's mouth. That's where Torika abandoned her. The sea raged with frantic waves, slamming her with promises of drowning.

I'm a stranger in Kalara's eyes. She will allow me to cross.

Wind lords spat in her face, but their breath carried her closer to the grieving frigate. Nina choked on unholy water and hoped for swift deliverance.

"Take the rope."

Nina blinked away rain and despair. A thick brown coil floated within her reach. She held tight with both hands.

"Hold on." Esiteri shouted.

Nina hooked her fingers around the ladder and scrambled up. She felt small and weak in her strange new body. The girl with rust-coloured hair leaned overboard.

"Take my hand, quick."

When they touched, the rain turned to exploding embers.

"What are you doing in the sea? Where's Nim?"

Nina's face was a labyrinth of wet hair, true answers lost somewhere in the middle.

"I...h-he's been replaced. I'm the new box collector."

"Your voice...look at me." Esiteri said, crouching between her legs. She lifted her chin with a finger.

"It can't be. Nina?"

The hope in her tone punched Nina in the heart.

I don't know your Nina. What she liked or who she was. What made her smile or what made her cry.

"It's me."

"Impossible…you're dead."

"I'm here now, with you. That's all that matters." Nina said, nose-booping her.

Esiteri beamed. The affectionate gesture transformed her face into a strange sunset.

"The gods heard my prayers. I thought I'd never see you again."

They kissed in a floating ember shower, passion bullets lodged deep in their hearts. Bodies hungered for familiar hands. Nina's lips brushed the pale canvas of Esiteri's stomach. She pulled down her leggings, grinning at the simple black panties that seemed too small for her. They were soaked with desire.

"Oh, Nina." she moaned, when her lover buried her nose in a red seagrass of hair—sweet waves crushing against her diligent tongue. Nina slipped a finger inside her, just one, remembering how small and tight she was. Intense heat radiated from her groin. Or so she thought.

Nina stopped and pulled away.

"What's the matter?"

"Something's happening. Can you feel the heat?"

"I sure can…" Esiteri said, giggling with eyes like mirrored seduction.

Smoke rose from her garments. "The embers…how did she know it was me?"

"What are you talking abo—"

The sentence died in her throat when Nina screamed. A hurricane of flames melted her skin. The ship sang a duet of caterwauls. Esiteri fought shock and panic but remained glued to the ground. Nina burned in a fiery globe, pain and gravity bringing her down eventually. Then stillborn silence.

———

Sirilo paced along the crab-littered shore. His heart-shaped pupils reflected a human inferno collapsing on the distant vessel. The sea hummed dead lullabies to a spectacle he witnessed too many times. He glanced to the east. Trailing tentacles signaled for his attention. Torika swam closer.

"My fellow shepherd. You seem bored." she said.

"Eternity in this endless nightmare, how can I not be?"

Torika's eyes rotated to the grieving ship. "He remembers nothing?"

"No. When he rises, the cycle will start all over again."

"I must admit, feeding him the same story over and over is tedious. I'm nobody's servant."

"We're all servants. That's what we do." Sirilo said, eating remains of his shed skin.

"Why is he even here?"

"A domino of murders. He betrayed his wife, she killed him and his lover, then his lover's girlfriend killed her and then herself."

The jellyfish tittered. "My sea is drowning in broken hearts. Nim's eternal punishment is a failure to win Esiteri's love? And Kalara's punishment is to watch her husband pine after the woman she hates, while Esiteri eternally grieves for Nina, whom she lost and is then reunited with, only for Kalara to burn her body—destroying the temporary happiness of her husband *and* his lover?"

Sirilo nodded.

"And they all remember nothing? This is too perfect."

The half-lizard began to retreat when fire called his name.

"Punishment by hope. It's a delicious torment."

———

Newborn flames delivered him to the grave of the now-known mariner. He crawled naked, baptized in confusion and melancholy. "Where am I?"

The bottled women in forsaken caverns sang an anthem for the lost. Clouds with brutish faces of imps frowned at him. They cried aborted embryos that crashed on his shoulders.

"Home." said the fire in Sirilo's voice.

A colony of child-eyed jellyfish lit the ocean's surface while he dressed in rags. The net—his instrument—was tucked behind whale bones. Violent stomach cramps chopped him down. Nim heaved behind a veil of sweat and regurgitated a dead crab.

"What is this?" he groaned.

"A delicacy, my friend. Feed on them and your dreams shall come true—if only for a moment." Sirilo said, his tail stroking a battered old container.

"You know, one of these days you'll tell me what's inside."

"Does it matter? Collecting these tins is the only way you get to see her."

The half-lizard flicked his tongue, a motion he barely registered. A circle of vomit smeared his mouth. Nimlesh kecked and glanced seaward, to the frigate and to the red-haired cargo that held his heart.

"But I want to speak to her."

He squatted and brushed fingers against the tinplate, its contents promising hopes of reunion.

The shepherd of Hell pushed the box aside, his skin-layered eyes shone with apathy.

"Impossible. She tosses, you fetch. That's how it's always been."

OTHER PUNISHMENTS

Redclover

THE KITCHEN REEKED OF SQUID AND TINNED frustration. Caratacos studied his coffee. A black lagoon where he often fished for answers. Cubes of squid heart like bait for the broken. Solitude and loneliness. The key to dreams and self-discovery. Principles of the chosen. He felt the weight of Gyda's glare on his shoulders.

"Máel is just a boy. Isolation will destroy his mind."

"There's nothing wrong with being alone." Caratacos said, thumbing his soul patch.

"There is if you're eleven-years-old. He's not like you, husband."

"He's not like anyone. That's why they ostracized him."

Gyda ripped off tentacles with conquered patience. "Children shun him because of his scar. They fear it."

"And so they should. Máel is destined for greatness. He must remain true to his path. No distractions."

She sliced the squid body into plump rings. Caratacos drank from the cup of inky stillness, his mind overturning thoughts like blank tarot cards. Words of a mother. Soothing. Nourishing. Weak. He understood the corruptive influence of others. Discipline and repetition. The formula of dying masters.

"You push him too hard." Gyda said.

"I'm pushing his dreams to reality. His name will not be forgotten. That I promise you."

"Your dreams, not his."

Caratacos sighed, vexation travelling on his breath.

"A life of mediocrity. Is that what you want for our son?"

"I want our son to be happy."

"Happiness is a myth. You feed him poisoned hope."

"I feed him love."

He leered in disgust. "Language of the frail."

For almost two decades Gyda shared his bed. Convenience masqueraded by wilting love. A corroded promise. His lust faded with her youth. Now her body was an abandoned playground. Old and rusty. Changed by the claw of time. Once a month, she rode him in the deepest midnight. Caratacos imagined Anah. Her skin warm like October rain. Wild. Magnetic. Fiery hair burning in cold moonlight.

"What is it, husband?"

Aching memories marked his face. Caratacos blinked away desires of her improbable return.

"He must train like his father and his father before him. Máel's character will be forged by solitude. Stop meddling, woman."

Caratacos. The lawmaker. Obstinate. Self-righteous.

"Our son needs friends. Someone to communicate with." Gyda said.

"He can talk to us. I will guide him. Always."

"There's more to this life than what you've known, husband."

Fist clashed with oak. Splinters pierced his skin. Raging sandstorm in unforgiving eyes. Caratacos trembled like a god of earthquakes.

"What do you know about my years of anguish?"

"Forgive me."

"This life was forced upon me, Gyda. I had no choice. Our parents cannot be chosen."

She bowed her head. The weight of sin greater than atlas-stones.

———

In the chamber beyond the wall, Máel punished his body. Three battles. Tendons strung in absolute tension. Three wars. Violent breaths like magmatic serpents. The ultimate truth. *One thousand days of training completes a beginner. Ten thousand days of training begins the mastery of the art.* Skeletal words of luckless fathers.

"Wanna play?"

The boy stopped.

"Toys are forbidden in this household. I have none."

Her tongue painted with extinct fruit spoke again: "I can be your toy."

Anah. The final ornament in his stark world.

"I can't play with you. The eye of Caratacos sees all."

"I am your friend."

"Friends are forbidden." Máel said.

She stripped out of the shadow mask that concealed her ageless eyes. A lifetime of wisdom earned with pain. They faced-off in a broken circle of dust. Ice-blue orbs swam along the length of his scar.

"The eye of your father is blinded by my cunt. Do not be afraid."

Pride straightened him. "I'm not afraid of you. You're just a girl."

Anah untied her robe and revealed a hungry triangle that enslaved tongues, cocks, and fingers.

"I am *your* girl and you can have me when the time comes."

Máel's child-heart pumped curiosity into his sex organ. Innocence besmirched by voices of awakened lust. Thoughts broken by a gentle melody of feminine knocks, then creaks of misaligned doors. Anah vanished into the ether. Only granular footprints remained. Gyda entered and lionized over the pyramid of her life.

"Who are you talking to, son?"

Máel veered. Fists clenched. Chest flexed. Tongue baking lies.

"No one."

"I heard voices."

"Only the sound of my breathing techniques."

She inspected all four corners of the chamber. Then the walls. Old and damaged. Like her.

"It's okay to talk to yourself when you're alone. I do sometimes. Your father is a hard man. He speaks with his eyes mostly."

"I don't talk to myself. I'm not that weak."

"It's not a weakness," she said.

"Words breed delay. In the pursuit of excellence, words have no home."

Gyda embraced her flesh and blood. The boy buried his nose into a scent of marine butchery. She raked curls of dark gold hair with broken nails.

"I know what haunts you, but the hammer of diligence will pummel your loneliness. Persevere, my son."

Máel unpeeled his face. The scar carved by the spear of Caratacos still burned bright. A reminder of misplaced trust.

"Yes, mother."

"You *must* succeed where your father has failed, do you hear?"

"I will."

"You were born from the ashes of his mistakes. A solitary hybrid of destruction. Now rise, my son. Let me see you."

The walls drummed. Sand-packed urns danced to rhythms of destiny. Máel imagined his future lover, Chaos. Mother's words pregnant with pride. Soothing. Nourishing. Weak. Caratacos warned him about misshapen words of foolish kin. *In the icy cave, you stand alone.*

———

The eye of Caratacos surveilled his dreams. A kaleidoscope of massacred children. Weak bones marinated in piss and mud and black smoke. War cries of blood-greedy hawks unchained a storm of tridents. Little bodies folded in queer but mesmeric angles. Amid chaos, Máel. Drunk on death and now baptized by tears of hysterical mothers. Wind brides sang his name. *Máel. Máel. Máel.*

"Wake up."

Bed linen clung to his back. Máel gulped stale air and semidarkness. Hysteria and disarray. Side by side. They taunted him.

"Why are you here?"

Anah spoke in otherworldly kisses. Comfort ferried by her tongue.

"Stop it. My training continues at dawn. I must dream."

"And I am the gate to your dreams, silly boy."

"He will punish us," Máel said.

"No. He will punish *you*."

"But you can protect me?"

A sabre of quietness pierced the shadows of her mouth. Anah roamed inside his mind-castle like a broken ghost.

"You don't need my protection. Your dreams are indestructible."

Máel said nothing. *You must succeed where your father has failed, do you hear?* The misconceived faith of ordinary mothers.

"I don't want to wake up."

"You fear the trial. Failure scares you." Anah said.

"I doubt myself. Doubt is the brother of fear."

Anah adopted his orphaned tear with a solitary kiss.

"Hearts. Alive. Say it."

Máel paused. "Do you promise?"

"Yes."

Her eyes glimmered like moonlit waves, drowning sacred words beneath his tongue.

"I cannot…"

"Trust in me. We are bound by fate. Say it."

The mango-sweet juice of her tongue was an antidote to poisoned reason. Máel raked his thoughts.

"The cave is like a thousand-piece jigsaw with nine-hundred and ninety-nine hidden pieces. I do not know what awaits me inside. Someone. Some*thing*. The trial ruined my father's life. What if I share his weakness?"

She peeled a nail from her little finger and plucked out a strand of fire-tinged hair.

"What are you doing?"

"You spawned from the venomous seed of Caratacos, but my essence will shield you from the all-consuming legacy of darkness."

Anah formed a loop and bound the nail. Hands of days unlived clamped his temples. Máel puffed. The nail became his father. Her hair became a lasso of magma. Scorched flesh bloomed between his teeth. Caratacos burned alive in his mind's eye.

"Vanquish your enemies. Eat."

Máel swallowed her gift. It tasted like powder of patriarchal bones.

"Will I survive?"

Sadness eclipsed her pale half-smile.

"In the icy cave, you stand alone. Choose wisely."

"And what if I don't?"

Their fingers rooted together.

"Face the trial. Then see."

"Don't make me wake up."

Anah breathed seeds of conviction into his barren soul.

"Hearts. Alive." he said.

———

Beneath mating skins of manta rays, Caratacos greeted the sun. In the ruins of circumcised promises, he dreamt.

"I'm ready, father."

Caratacos spun. The scarred face of redemption blinded him.

"Máel. Your journey begins. Can you conquer snake's whisper?"

"Yes, father."

"And the coast of ore. You know wherein it lies?"

The last son of Caratacos nodded. *Beyond the fallen obelisk and herd of scales.*

"Good. Crawl along grieving sand dunes for three days and stay away from crucified waves. Never sleep inside her mouth."

Cheap words and cryptic meanings.

"Yes, father."

Their eyes dueled. Pride versus shame. Caratacos felt the bruise in his heart.

"Do not fail me, my son. Listen to the dying songs of fallen meteors, but when the time comes—shield your compassion."

Máel's face was a dynasty of aborted emotions. A trigold painted cloud ingested the sun below. Combers licked faraway cliffs.

"I will, father."

The satchel unbalanced his shoulders. Gyda rationed provisions for seventy-two hours. Perhaps enough for a sole journey.

"Go now." Caratacos said.

The white shadows uttered no words of his return.

———

Squid meat fed his stomach, but Anah fed his heart. He remembered her eyes. How they sang lustful hymns under naked sky. Sand fleas licked his skin red. Máel squirmed like a human worm under burning glass. *The waves. They burn. I can't.* A chasm of expired backbones reserved his name. Máel was dying. Strong body operated by feeble will. Glory, drowned. Promises, forgotten. On a crimson seabed, they crucified him. Anah's breath travelled in sad clouds.

Her spider silk arms broke his fall from the eye of Caratacos.

"Look at me."

The voice of a wounded angel. Under ore-soul bridge she offered her breast. Máel groaned and tilted his head, greedy lips glued to a lavish pink nipple.

"Stop."

He paused. Anah's freckled face glowed with a light of thousand asteroids. Time restructured her bones. She was a woman now.

"Is that really you?"

Anah kissed him behind a flame-haired veil and he tasted mangos again. When their mouths separated, he glimpsed the scale of her well-travelled tongue.

"How long?" he said.

"Nights. Days. Centuries."

A caged heart whispered aching words. She extended her hand. Their fingertips danced together to a melody of savage desire. Máel struggled to unlock his memories. *Hydropain. She rescued me from the wrath of crucified waves.* Reality scratched him.

"I failed. It's over."

Anah yawned and caution tightened his body. A shelter from a bad world. Temptation, unbound. *Never sleep inside her mouth.* Voiceless fathers. Tricksters.

"No. It's beginning." she said.

———

Máel kneeled in the cavern of ice. In the glacier's mirror, his face slept. He was a man now. Regal. Caratacos redefined. She waited on the alter built from bones of lovers past. Exotic ink flowed beneath her skin.

In the icy cave, you stand alone. Path of the fool. Anah parted her legs.

"I said you could have me when the time comes. Drink."

She pressed his mouth to her hot spring. The taste of urine and nameless fluids. Trained like his father and his father before him. Tantalizing-blue eyes. Wild. Magnetic. Flawless curves and intense charisma. Skin warm like October rain. A salacious rivulet flowed between father and son. Borrowed desire, inherited weakness.

"Play with me," she said.

Harp fingers switched with his tongue. Erratic heartbeats and bestial moans. Máel probed inside her sugar walls.

"The spear of Caratacos. Let me see."

He disrobed. Webbed-fingers still smeared with her love.

"Hearts. Alive. Say it."

Anah rode him in the deepest midnight.

"Hearts. Alive."

———

In the chamber beyond the wall, he awoke. Sparrow-like claw mauled his spear. Máel gasped, exhausted.

"So easily manipulated," said the deformity named Anah, "you could resist everything but temptation."

Barbed tail bound his body, eyes ablaze. Words of a father. Sooth-ing. Nourishing. Weak.

"Leave me be, she-demon. I must prepare for the trial."

Anah's cackle sub-zeroed his heart. He knew what she was about to say.

Tender Whisper On A Crimson Tongue

"Shadows bleed." I say.

Your heart shelters pity—an orphanage for unwanted love. You watch Maddie lick my skin. A ritual of old wisdom. Her kiss summons pain and you almost protest. Inherited blood rises from a re-opened wound. The colour of a vulgar lipstick.

"You cut too deep."

Maddie and I know true intimacy. She's a tender whisper on a crimson tongue. I invite her deeper. Your expression changes to pregnant sorrow.

"Leon, please."

My eyes linger on your fading tattoo. A black and grey outline of a heart pierced by a woeful dagger. I wonder who stabbed your heart and how many hearts you've stabbed in return.

"Lemme enrich that colour," I stir my fingers in a palette of skin and blood, "lemme breathe life into your pale heart."

You flinch away from me. Like I'm a piranha in a river of stillbirths. Your intense gaze falls on Maddie. She stares back.

"Drop the razor, Leon."

You think you know me, but I refuse to betray Maddie. Her silver

touch makes me feel alive. A complex relationship built on founda-
tions of mute discretion and sharp comfort.

"We are here for the same reason. I won't die, don't worry."

You kneel beside me. Teardrops falling like ancient civilizations. I
adore the smallness of your feet. Delicate and pastel-white.

"Stop. Think of Freya. She won't benefit from your death if you cut
too deep."

Your words don't move me. Only the language of your eyes.
Galvanic affection swirling in a wave of punishing blue. I caress your
freckled face and your hair glows like dying embers. Rivulets of blood
parachute to the grave-cold ground.

"Shadows bleed." I say again.

The room smells of burnt parchment and wasted lives. There are two
beds, but I'm alone. Almost. Maddie sleeps in my pocket. She wakes
and punishes me for what I lost. For what I am. Cold teeth tease inked
runes around my wrist. An unbearable tension pulses beneath.
Maddie bites. Relief wrapped in dark blood, blossoming together. You
enter my ash-smeared world on the fourth night. Your face is a chart
of bewilderment. Like you're sharing a cage with a broken animal. You
contemplate turning back.

"Stay." I say.

Maddie bares her teeth, still tinged with my bleeding regrets.

"Why are you cutting yourself?"

Your voice is croaky. Alcohol sings in your veins. I seal the wound
with a cheap plaster.

"I'm feeding shadows."

I finger-point at the untouched bed. Heavy duty. Military issued.

"What's your name?" you ask, sinking opposite me.

"Leon."

Silence trampolines from my lips. You're waiting, wondering why I
haven't asked. The truth is—your name is meaningless. I'm here to die.

"How long you've been in this place?"

"Four days." I say.

"And how long does it take?"

I blame alcohol for blunting your mind. My face is a festival of sadness.

"I'm still here. I don't know."

"That's crazy. No consssistency then?"

Your lisp is betrayed by ill chosen words. I grin and you blush like a clumsy ballerina.

"My tongue is too big for my mouth."

"Alright."

I feign indifference, yet adoration hooks my heart.

"I need a drink." you say.

Your large tongue teases behind fluorescent teeth, baiting me. I saunter across the room in slippers made from cold shadows. The cabinet is well-stocked.

"What would you like?"

You rummage in an unbranded rucksack. Layers of dark charisma are reinforced by the small, horizontal scar in the corner of your left eye.

"Something that gets me drunk."

I nod and reach for a bottle of absinthe from a country I can't remember the name of. I feel your eyes on me. Maddie-sharp and guileful. I don't read the label.

"Taste this hellfire." I say, pouring you two fingers.

"Thanks."

I glance at your lips, coloured like morganite. They welcome alcohol with mad urgency. A ravening gulp and you smile at the cloudy bottom.

"Mmm, devilishly good."

You raise your glass for a refill, but your eyes drink me instead. I feel like you undress my soul. The sound of flowing absinthe distracts you.

"Get drunk with me, Leon. We might be dead tomorrow."

You swallow liquor like Maddie swallows blood.

"Does your savior have a name?" I say.

"What do you mean?"

I sit beneath your feet in half-lotus like a love-sick disciple.

"Maddie is my razor blade. She drinks my pain. What do you call your savior?"

"Captain Morgan. We shared many voyages together."

You salute me, then the green fairy disappears down that sensual mouth I so badly want to taste.

"How long have you been cutting yourself?" you say.

There's no point in hiding the truth. It will never leave this base. We'll burst into the black sky and only stars will sing at our funeral.

"I was a human totem in my village."

"What do you mean?"

You repeat those four words more than any other combination.

"Drunk old men believed that if they carved certain symbols into my skin—the gate would open. Well, they thought that I would open."

I drop my gaze to your girlish shoulders, then to your tartan pants and Doc Martens, and back up to that mischievous grin. I instantly gravitate to your energy. I thrive on it.

"The gate to what?"

"To something—"

A soldier barges in. I don't know his name or rank. He's tall and unarmed and ordinary. His face is stained with authority and something like gratitude.

"Afternoon. It's time. Thank you once again for helping us study what exactly happens to bomb victims. We're making valuable progress here, thanks to people like you."

————

You and I greet dark sun together, hand in hand. I glimpse two bomb chairs in a graveyard of lost body parts. I close my eyes and imagine when they detonate us. A vicious rain of limbs. If only we met under different circumstances. In another life, I know I could love you.

Micro-Poems

A CHAMELEON DRESSED

in your eyelashes
gave birth to a
red star

---

singing pale
breaths to
a drowning
anchor
he sank
like martyred
daughters

---

she wrote
ruby-clad
scars
on the
torn
parchment
of
his skin

---

a jellyfish spurned
and floating
in hidden tears
below
lamenting lost
lovers
like he did

Red stone
skimming across
the rust-kissed
surface of
my soul

Mist of lost
orphans
veiled her
abandoned
eyes

She was a heart
note in
the
perfume
of swan
tears

Leviathan's tongue
skewered
by a broken
rib
her eyes
like wet scales
in a sea of

eternity

Tumbling emotions
in an iris of blue
changing
fading
ghosts of you

A febrile crow
and unspoken oaths
lonesome
nights
a vortex of delirious
memories

I slept on a raft of snakes
echoes of obstinate words
barring me
from the warm blue waters
of your eyes
my haven

Your lips
coloured like
morganite
welcoming alcohol
with
mad urgency

Stray raindrops
tap against
my cold window
pleading

Pale tears

and broken
heartstrings when
she sang

Eskimo kisses
in
a porcelain
glow

Like a rogue tribe
of fire-tinged stones
she rolled down
my heart

---

her eyes
smudged with seduction
and
enigmatic
blue

---

frost gods
whispered perversions
thawed
by
time

---

the sleeping sun
below
his feet
dreamed of black
rain

---

stillborn firestars
burned
like choleric

sinners

---

lyrics of violent death
painted scarlet
letters into
the
midnight
sky

Dive into the Decadence:

AN ESSAY ON "PUNISHMENT BY HOPE" BY MIKE ARNZEN

GET READY. THIS IS NOT A NORMAL STORY.

Which is not to say that it is "abnormal" -- though the grim and graphic sexuality of this tale definitely puts it on the other side of the norm.

And though it is definitely "paranormal," with all its depiction of demons and shepherds in an oceanic hell, there is something else that makes it more than just another sick erotic/gothic/WTF story from Erik Hofstatter.

No, the word that comes to mind for me is "lyrical." Which, sadly, is not what you "normally" find in today's literary culture at all anymore.

"Punishment by Hope" is foremost concerned with using the musicality of language in getting you to feel something. In other words, the style is poetic -- which is a refreshing thing to read in a world so centered on novels and common, easily digestible prose. Hofstatter wields a verb with flair, keeping his sentences tight and direct. Sometimes they sting. Sometimes they settle in. Sometimes they suck you down. Sometimes they soar.

"Punishment by Hope" ebbs and flows in its oceanic imagery, giving you a taste of something you might want before churning in gore or the grotesque and then withdrawing back into its own uncanny depths like some kind of foamy blood tide. And like the vast ocean, the tale it spins is at once visceral, lustrous and literally unfathomable. You will likely be enthralled as you're pulled into its painful and prurient undertow, but also more than a little confused because what you're given here is the effect without the cause, whereas most narrative stories walk you step by step from cause to effect over and over again.

It might even frustrate you. But that's okay, because this is a story about frustration. And be prepared, because Hofstatter is going to challenge you on many levels. The poetry of Hofstatter's style conjures the imagery in your mind as much as the carefully-chosen words will, evoking emotion first. The logic behind what you are experiencing -- which you will only receive a glimpse of at the tale's climax -- is a side-effect that would otherwise only be reductive if it dominated the story.

Some pages of this book will be filled with white space, with a string of brief one-sentence paragraphs that read quite literally like lines of poetry, delivering the deep dialogue like waves lapping a shore. You have to dip your toes in it, frightful as it may be, and let the feeling wash over you, wave after wave. Some of those waves will send chills up your leg. Others might make you wretch or want to turn away, wondering just what kind of waters you are soaking in, and whether these waves will wreck you. Enjoy. You'll find you're fully submerged anyway, if you make it deep enough into the story.

On top of the poetic style and the morbidly romantic tone, the book harkens to its literary forefathers who also are poets. It ultimately belongs to the legacy of "decadent" literature, which means it echoes the writing of 19th century literary libertines (by authors like Baudelaire) who were interested in foregoing realism and being playfully extravagant with their language in order to explore the liberty of desire and give credit to the passions which are otherwise censored or held back by realistic forms of representation. But beyond that, you might also detect references to Dante's "Inferno" in the way Nim is led through this world of torment by Hell's shepherd. Or you might think of Coleridge's "Rime of the Ancient Mariner" in the allusions to albatrosses and water, hope and memory and loss. These are poetic, lyrical predecessors, mashed up with some modern day obscenity. Hofstatter's horror storytelling is not drawing from the common stock of King or McCammon or even Poe, though it has touches of the latter in its lyrical nature, in much the same way Clive Barker does, delving into the taboos of desire. Only the writing here is more lyrical than Clive Barker's work. This is raw nightmare, in poetic form.

As I've said, this is more concerned with evoking emotion than relying on the logic of any of it, because the story -- the origin of Nim's fate -- is but a mere explanation that ultimately cannot adequately explain anything at all. The "punishment by hope" that the title refers to is really, in the end, another name for "unrequited love" -- which is something of a romantic trap and a cliche of poetic literature, but here it is framed as a kind of hell of senselessness -- a hell that words cannot contain or do justice to -- a hell that the protagonist is trapped inside and cannot fully comprehend.

But emotions can at least get a reader to identify on a deep level. We are invited to see ourselves experiencing the emotional longing of the protagonist here, even if some of his memories are despicable, even if (as we discover at the end) he is responsible for a lot of what makes him suffer, and with good reason. He is tormented by his own sin, which is driven by a dark lust as much as love. He gets what he deserves. Which -- spoiler alert -- is nothing but nightmare.

Given the climate of today's literary scene, I know some readers will find the obscenity in this story as something overly masculinist, or that the author is "going for the gross out" in an exploitative or unredeeming way -- and though all good horror should repulse us a little bit, such a response would do this short story a disservice. I've read enough "edge lit" and "avant punk" and bizarro horror fiction across my lifetime to recognize this as a moral allegory for existential pain, drawing from the tradition of decadent literature that's been exploring social taboos and the desire of the human animal for more than 100 years -- and I hope Hofstatter's readers will, too.

If not, there is little hope for them, and banality shall be their eternal punishment.

An ocean siren is calling. Shoes off. Time to take a dip...

-- Michael Arnzen, Pittsburgh, 2020

Dear Reader,

We hope you enjoyed reading *Punishment by Hope*. Please take a moment to leave a review, even if it's a short one. Your opinion is important to us.

Discover more books by Erik Hofstatter at
    https://www.nextchapter.pub/authors/erik-hofstatter

Want to know when one of our books is free or discounted? Join the newsletter at
    http://eepurl.com/bqqB3H

Best regards,

Erik Hofstatter and the Next Chapter Team

Lightning Source UK Ltd.
Milton Keynes UK
UKHW011849080221
378458UK00001B/197

9 781034 381389